DATE DUE			

NOV   2003

GREAT MOMENTS IN BASKETBALL

by Michael Burgan

WORLD ALMANAC® LIBRARY

Please visit our web site at: www.worldalmanaclibrary.com
For a free color catalog describing World Almanac® Library's
list of high-quality books and multimedia programs,
call 1-800-848-2928 (USA) or 1-800-387-3178 (Canada).
World Almanac® Library's fax: (414) 332-3567.

Library of Congress Cataloging-in-Publication Data

Burgan, Michael.
    Great moments in basketball / by Michael Burgan. — North American ed.
       p. cm. — (Great moments in sports)
    Summary: Recounts ten high points in the history of basketball, including Wilt Chamberlain's
100-point game, eight consecutive NBA championships won by the Boston Celtics, and the Houston
Comets win the first four WNBA championships.
    Includes bibliographical references and index.
    ISBN 0-8368-5345-8 (lib. bdg.)
    ISBN 0-8368-5359-8 (softcover)
    1. Basketball—United States—History—Juvenile literature. [1. Basketball—History.] I. Title.
II. Great moments in sports (Milwaukee, Wis.)
GV885.1.B87   2002
796.323'0973—dc21
                                              2002016875

This North American edition first published in 2002 by
World Almanac® Library
330 West Olive Street, Suite 100
Milwaukee, WI 53212 USA

This U.S. edition © 2002 by World Almanac® Library.

An Editorial Directions book
Editor: Lucia Raatma
Photo researcher: Image Select International Ltd.
Copy editor: Melissa McDaniel
Proofreader: Sarah De Capua
Indexer: Tim Griffin
Art direction, design, and page production: The Design Lab
World Almanac® Library editorial direction: Mark J. Sachner
World Almanac® Library art direction: Tammy Gruenewald
World Almanac® Library production: Susan Ashley and Jessica L. Yanke

Photographs ©: Getty Images, cover, 3, 5; Associated Press, 6; Getty Images, 7; Associated Press,
8; Corbis, 9, 10, 11, 12, 13; Getty Images, 14, 15 top, 15 bottom, 16, 18; Corbis, 19; Getty
Images, 20; Corbis, 21; Getty Images, 22; Corbis, 23 top; Getty Images, 23 bottom; Corbis, 25,
26, 27 top, 28 bottom, 29; Getty Images, 30, 31, 32, 33, 34, 35; AFP, 36, 37; Corbis, 38; Allsport,
39; Reuters/Popperfoto, 40; Getty Images, 41, 42, 43; AFP, 44; Getty Images, 45; Associated Press,
46 top left; Corbis, 46 bottom left; Getty Images, 46 left.

Printed in the United States of America

1 2 3 4 5 6 7 8 9 06 05 04 03 02

Opposite: *Shaquille O'Neal has established himself
as the L.A. Lakers' prime playoff motivator.*

Contents

Introduction

To go in for a ferocious slam dunk, dish off a no-look pass, or fake out a defender with a tricky piece of dribbling, the best basketball players need a variety of skills. Talented players and a fast pace have made basketball one of the world's most popular sports. Today, "hoops" is played in more than two hundred countries, and professional leagues for both men and women exist on almost every continent.

This international sport has American roots. In 1891, James Naismith, a physical education teacher in Springfield, Massachusetts, came up with a new indoor sport to keep his students active during the winter. He took two peach baskets and put one at each end of the gym, then gave his students a soccer ball. Naismith's idea was to throw the ball into the basket, so his new game was eventually called basketball.

At first, basketball was low scoring. A typical final score might be 4–3. Play stopped after each goal so someone could remove the ball from the basket, and until the introduction of the backboard in 1896, fans

in the stands could swat away shots. Rules changed over time, and women used different rules than men. One major difference: a women's court was divided into three separate areas. Players were assigned to a particular area and could not leave it during the game. Today, rules for men's and women's games are more similar than in the past.

During basketball's early years, college hoops won the most attention from fans and the media. By the 1930s, thousands of fans often filled New York's Madison Square Garden for college basketball doubleheaders. College players are also given credit for introducing the jump shot and making the dunk a common play.

Professional leagues began to form in 1898, but none of them lasted long. More popular were barnstormers—pro teams that traveled around the country playing any team that challenged them. Today's major pro league began as the Basketball Association of America in 1946 and became the National Basketball Association (NBA) three years later, making it the youngest of the leagues in the four major team sports (baseball, football, basketball, and hockey).

In 1954, the NBA introduced an important new element to the game: the shot clock. Before then, a team could hold onto the ball as long as it

The ultimate in home-court advantage and birthplace of Celtic Pride: the parquet floor, championship banners, and retired numbers adorning the old Boston Garden, where the Celtics built one of sport's most fabled dynasties.

wanted before shooting. The shot clock has sped up the pace of the game and increased scoring. In college ball, women began using a shot clock in 1969, while the men added it in 1985.

A few pro leagues for women started up during the 1970s, but they all failed. At the college level, women's basketball became more popular during the 1990s, and the U.S. women's victory at the 1996 Summer Olympics also boosted the sport.

In 1997, the NBA started a pro league for women, the Women's National Basketball Association (WNBA). This league has done well, attracting the finest women players from around the world and drawing thousands of fans per game.

During its history, basketball has had many extraordinary players and great moments. Some of these moments can happen in a single game; others stretch out over a season or cap a career. Choosing only ten for this book was difficult. Some achievements are so great, no one would argue whether they should be included here. Other great moments, however, are not so clear-cut. Basketball's historic high points—from the pros and college, for men and women—could fill several books like this one. Here is one view of ten great moments in basketball.

THE BIG DIPPER HITS A HUNDRED

Wilt Chamberlain Scores One Hundred Points in One Game

When Wilt "the Stilt" Chamberlain entered the NBA in 1959, he was known as a powerful defensive force. At 7 feet 1 inch (216 centimeters) and 275 pounds (125 kilograms), this dominating center could swat aside shots or make opponents think twice about cutting to the basket. But Chamberlain left his

Chamberlain celebrates his achievement in the locker room following his record-breaking game.

true mark on the game as a scorer. Even superstar Michael Jordan could not top many of the

scoring records Chamberlain set.

As a rookie, Chamberlain led the league in scoring with 37.6 points per game. Before him, no NBA player had ever averaged more than thirty. He was also the league's leading scorer the next six years, with his best season coming in 1961–1962. Playing for the Philadelphia Warriors, Chamberlain averaged an amazing 50.4 points per game; no other player has ever averaged more than forty. The highlight of that special season came on March 2, 1962, as "the Big Dipper" and his teammates met the New York Knicks.

Small Crowd for a Big Game

The two teams met at an arena in Hershey, Pennsylvania, where the Warriors sometimes played. Before the game, Chamberlain played a target-shooting game in the arena lobby. That night, he rarely missed. It was, he later said, "an omen of things to come."

The Hershey arena had 7,200 seats, but only about four thousand people showed up for the game. The season was almost over, and the game meant nothing in the standings. The Warriors were already guaranteed a playoff spot, while the Knicks were stuck in last place. Chamberlain, who hadn't slept the night before, was loose during warm-ups. He laughed and sang along to a song playing in the arena. The record was called "By the River," and the singer was . . . Wilt Chamberlain—his one and only attempt at a singing career.

After the tip-off, the Warriors jumped out to a 19–3 lead. Chamberlain was hot from the start, hitting seven of fourteen shots in the first quarter. More impressive was his free-throw shooting, as he went a perfect nine for nine. Chamberlain struggled at the free-throw line his entire career, but on that night, he had a golden touch.

Throughout his career, Chamberlain played serious defense as well as dominating offense. Here he tries to prevent a scoring drive by Bill Russell of the Boston Celtics.

At halftime, the Warriors led 79–68. Chamberlain already had forty-one points. In the second half, he continued to score easily, with many of his baskets coming on fadeaway jumpers. By the end of the third quarter, he had sixty-nine, bringing him close to a record that he already held—most points in a game. Before the 1961–1962 season, the record was seventy-one, but Chamberlain had scored seventy-eight for the Warriors earlier in the season.

"Give It to Wilt!"

As the game went on, fans began chanting for the Warriors to pass the ball to Chamberlain, and his teammates obliged. To try to stop the massive center, the Knicks defenders crowded around him, fouling him almost every time he touched the ball. Then they fouled the other Warriors, so they couldn't get the ball to Chamberlain. Still, he kept pouring in points. With each basket, the arena announcer gave Chamberlain's point total, so everyone knew when he broke the old

Wilt Chamberlain scoring his one-hundredth point in a history-making game against the New York Knicks on March 3, 1962.

scoring record. The fans chanted for more: "We want 100, we want 100!" Chamberlain later said, "I thought, 'Man these fans are tough. Eighty isn't good enough. I'm tired. I've got 80 points and no one has ever scored 80.'" Chamberlain, though, stayed in the game and kept scoring.

With 1:19 to play, Chamberlain reached ninety-eight points with a dunk. About thirty seconds later, the Warriors had the ball again and Chamberlain received a pass. Some people

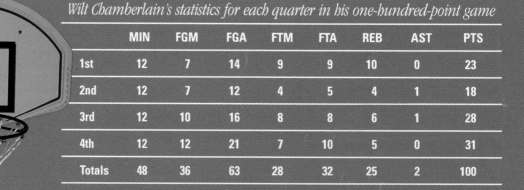

BY THE NUMBERS

Wilt Chamberlain's statistics for each quarter in his one-hundred-point game

	MIN	FGM	FGA	FTM	FTA	REB	AST	PTS
1st	12	7	14	9	9	10	0	23
2nd	12	7	12	4	5	4	1	18
3rd	12	10	16	8	8	6	1	28
4th	12	12	21	7	10	5	0	31
Totals	48	36	63	28	32	25	2	100

who were at the arena say he then moved to the basket and dunked. Others say he went for a lay-up. Chamberlain couldn't remember later what shot he took. But he knew the ball went in, giving him one hundred points. The fans rushed the court to congratulate Chamberlain, and it took the referees five minutes to get them off and play the last few seconds.

The final score was 169–147 for the Warriors. Chamberlain played the entire forty-eight minutes of that historic game. He made twenty-eight free throws, the most ever for a single game, and set a record for most points in a half with fifty-nine. The future Hall of Famer finished the season with 4,029 points, a record no other player has approached. Chamberlain, who died in 1999, will always be remembered for that incredible season and especially for his one-hundred-point game.

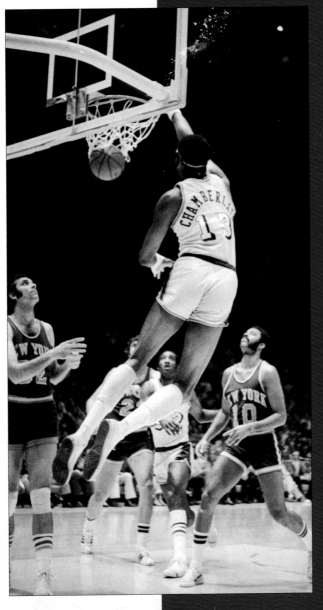

A HIGH AND LOW POINT

After scoring one hundred points, Wilt Chamberlain was excited about his great accomplishment. As the years went by, however, he had a different view. In the book *Tall Tales*, a collection of interviews with former NBA players, Chamberlain had this to say about the game:

The 100-point game will never be as important to me as it is to some other people. That's because I'm embarrassed by it. After I got into the 80s, I pushed for 100 and it destroyed the game because I took shots that I normally never would. I was not real fluid. I mean, 63 shots? You take that many shots on a playground and no one ever wants you on their team again. . . . I've had many better games than this one, games where I scored 50–60 points and shot 75 percent.

Later in his career, Chamberlain brought his scoring skills to the Los Angeles Lakers.

TRIPLE THREAT

Oscar Robertson Averages a Triple-Double for a Season

A triple-double is one of the greatest individual feats in basketball. A player needs tremendous all-around talent to reach double figures in scoring, rebounding, and assists. Larry Bird and Magic Johnson were modern masters of the triple-double, each doing it more than fifty times during their careers. The greatest of all time, however, was Oscar Robertson. His 178 career triple-doubles are still a record, and in NBA history, only "the Big O" has ever averaged a triple-double over an entire season.

"The Big O"—a talented ball handler and all-around classy player.

Early Talent

Robertson joined the Cincinnati Royals in 1960 after an amazing college career at the University of Cincinnati. For three consecutive years, he was the national college player of the year and the leading scorer. He finished his college career averaging almost thirty-four points per game and held the record for career points, with 2,973. At 6 feet 5 inches (196 cm) Robertson was also an excellent rebounder, averaging fifteen boards per game through college.

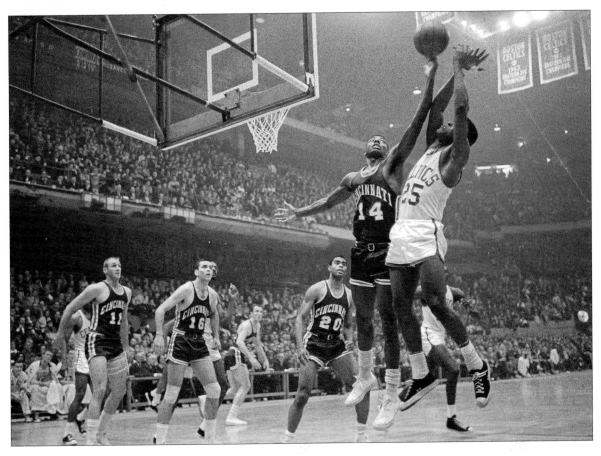

After a standout college stint at the University of Cincinnati, Robertson continued his career in Cincinnati with the Royals.

As a rookie with the Royals, Robertson switched from forward to guard. At that position, he had a chance to use his ball-handling and passing skills. Robertson quickly showed that he was one of the most complete players in the NBA. Boston Celtics coach Red Auerbach later said, "There's nothing Oscar can't do. He's so great, he scares me."

BY THE NUMBERS

Oscar Robertson's major statistics for his triple-double season and his near misses

	G	REB	AST	PTS	REB AVG	AST AVG	PTS AVG
1960–1961	71	716	690	2,165	10.1	9.7	30.5
1961–1962	79	985	899	2,432	12.5	11.4	30.8
1962–1963	80	835	758	2,264	10.4	9.5	28.3
1963–1964	79	783	868	2,480	9.9	11.0	31.4
1964–1965	75	674	861	2,279	9.0	11.5	30.4
Totals	384	3,993	4,076	11,620	10.4	10.6	30.3

Oscar Robertson in action against Detroit Pistons Gene Shue and Chuck Noble.

His first season, Robertson averaged 30.5 points per game, third-best in the league. He also averaged 10.1 rebounds. He later said, "I came into the NBA with the idea that I was there to rebound, too. That was part of my job." So was making precise passes so his teammates could score easy hoops. Robertson led the league with 9.7 assists per game, leaving him just short of the triple-double for the season. He was an obvious choice for Rookie of the Year, and he also won the most valuable player (MVP) award for the All-Star game.

The Season

The next year, Robertson's first game showed what was to come the rest of the season. Playing against the St. Louis Hawks, he scored thirty-five points, grabbed fifteen rebounds, and handed out thirteen assists. Robertson shot just nine for twenty-seven from the field, but he made up for that by making seventeen out of nineteen free throws. As the season went on, he had more than a few games in which he took twenty-five or thirty shots, a tendency that led some players to call him a ball hog. But as opposing coach Dick

McGuire noted, "He'll make sure that each of the Royals gets a bucket in the first couple of minutes . . . the only time he'll concentrate on shooting is when they're behind."

Robertson turned in three more triple-doubles before his first "off night," when he pulled down only seven rebounds against the New York Knicks. Still, he scored thirty-seven points in that game, along with handing out thirteen assists. As the year went on, Robertson had several stellar games. At Philadelphia in November, he had a season-high twenty-two rebounds and forty-nine points in a loss to the Warriors. On Christmas Day against the Los Angeles Lakers, he scored forty, pulled down twelve rebounds, and dished seventeen assists. During a thirty-six-point performance against the Hawks, he hit a perfect eighteen for eighteen from the free-throw line.

For the Royals, the 1961–1962 season was disappointing, as they lost in the first round of the playoffs. For the Big O, however, the season was sensational. He finished averaging 30.8 points per game, third-best in the league, and he scored in double figures every game. His 11.4 assists average was best in the NBA, making him the first player ever to average in double figures for that category. Robertson also had a 12.5 rebounding average, completing the season-long triple-double. The only player to come close to duplicating that accomplishment? Oscar Robertson.

PLAYING THE TOTAL GAME

After he retired, Oscar Robertson shared his thoughts on the triple-double:

The triple-double is blown out of proportion. No one noticed it when I played. Today, they are so cheap. An assist used to be a pass that led to a basket without a dribble. Now, you pass to a guy, he takes a dribble, makes a 25-footer, and that's an assist. Guys worry about getting one more rebound or assist for the triple-double—it's ridiculous. What matters is a guy who plays the total game. He's not after stats, but because that's how you should play the game, period.

Robertson and the Celtics' Bill Russell fighting for a rebound.

THE BEST TEAM EVER

The Boston Celtics Win Eight Consecutive NBA Championships

During the early years of the NBA, the Minneapolis Lakers were the league's dominant team, winning five championships in six years. Starting in the 1956–1957 season, however, a new dynasty emerged. That season, the Boston Celtics added rookie center Bill Russell to their lineup. He was the missing piece, the one player the Celtics needed to go from good to great. Over the next thirteen seasons, the Celtics won eleven championships,

Bill Russell—remembered as a truly remarkable talent on a remarkable Celtics team.

including an amazing eight in a row. Russell and a cast of other future Hall of Famers took the Celtics beyond great, compiling a winning tradition that no other NBA team has ever approached.

Red and the Gang

Along with great players, the Celtics had a skilled coach. With his trademark cigar and fiery temper, Red Auerbach was one of the most colorful personalities in the NBA. He developed a fast-paced game for the

Coach Red Auerbach, considered by many the architect of Celtic Pride, brought his legendary leadership to the players—and to the entire Celtics organization.

By 1956, the Celtics were good enough to make the playoffs, but not to win it all. After losing to Syracuse, Auerbach said, "With the talent we've got on this ball club, if we can come up with one big man to get us the ball, we'll win everything in sight." Auerbach had a big man in mind—Russell, who had dominated college ball while playing at the University of San Francisco. A lean 6 feet 9 inches (206 cm), Russell was a defensive specialist. In an era before blocked-shots

Celtics, built around grabbing defensive rebounds and racing down the court for a fast break. He also stressed team play—no Celtic ever won the league scoring title during the team's championship streak. Auerbach knew how to choose the right players for the team, then make them play to the best of their ability.

Despite his talents, Auerbach made a mistake in 1950 when he decided not to draft Bob Cousy. A dazzling passer, Cousy was the Magic Johnson of his day. Cousy ended up with the Celtics by accident, as his former team folded and the league split up the players among the other teams. Along with Bill Sharman, "the Cooz" was part of the best backcourt in basketball during the 1950s. Sharman was the outside shooter, while Cousy set up his teammates for easy hoops.

Point guard Bob Cousy, "The Houdini of the Hardwood," was the epitome of excellence throughout his storied career as a Boston Celtic.

statistics were kept, observers guessed that Russell averaged eight to ten blocks per game. He also hit the boards with skill and could score when necessary. To get Russell, Auerbach traded all-star Ed Macauley and promising rookie Cliff Hagan. Soon it was obvious the Celtics had gotten the best of the deal.

Along with Russell, the Celtics added forwards Tom Heinsohn and Frank Ramsey for the 1956–1957 season. This new lineup helped the Celtics win their first NBA championship, beating the St. Louis Hawks in seven games. The next season, Sam Jones joined the Celtics, and the team once again reached the finals. This time, the Hawks beat the Celtics, winning in six games. The spring of 1958 was the last time the Celtics watched another team celebrate the championship for many years.

John Havlicek contributed versatility, stamina, and heart to the Celtics' cause.

The Streak Begins

In 1958–1959, the Celtics' stars were Cousy, Sharman, Russell, and Heinsohn. The team

also had a rookie named K. C. Jones (no relation to Sam). Boston went 52–20 during the regular season, and in the finals, they romped over the Lakers, four games to none. The next year, the lineup was virtually unchanged, and so was the result at the end of the season. St. Louis played well in the finals, but the Celtics held on to win. The 1960–1961 season was the last for Bill Sharman, and he helped the Celtics win their third straight title, once again defeating the Hawks. After the final victory, Auerbach said, "This is the greatest team ever assembled. . . . We've always got somebody ready to explode. Any one of them can tear you apart." Not many people debated Auerbach's claim.

During the next several seasons, new players joined the team, and the Celtics kept winning. One of the most important arrivals was John Havlicek. "Hondo," as he was called, became the best sixth man in the game, the spark off the bench who added instant offense or made a key defensive stop. Havlicek is also famous in Celtics history for a steal he made during the last game of the 1965 Eastern Conference finals. His last-second swipe preserved a win against the Philadelphia 76ers. Boston then defeated the Los Angeles Lakers for its seventh consecutive championship. The next year, the Celtics and Lakers met again in the finals, and Boston won the championship one more time.

The streak finally ended in 1967, as Wilt Chamberlain led the 76ers to victory against Boston in the conference finals. That was also Auerbach's last year as coach. After that, he took over as general manager and named Russell as coach. Russell was a player-coach for several seasons, and in 1968 and 1969, he led the Celtics to two more league titles. After 1969, Russell retired, marking the end of the Celtics dynasty. Later, Russell said the Celtics were a family, "a family bent on winning."

BY THE NUMBERS

The Boston Celtics' record in the NBA finals during their streak of eight consecutive championships

Year	Opponent	Result
1959	Minneapolis Lakers	4–0
1960	St. Louis Hawks	4–3
1961	St. Louis Hawks	4–1
1962	Los Angeles Lakers	4–3
1963	Los Angeles Lakers	4–2
1964	San Francisco Warriors	4–1
1965	Los Angeles Lakers	4–1
1966	Los Angeles Lakers	4–3

THE WINNING WIZARD

UCLA Wins Eighty-eight Straight

The skyhook, college-style: The incomparable Kareem Abdul-Jabbar, then known as Lew Alcindor, goes up against Providence College.

Coach John Wooden had an easy explanation for his success at the University of California at Los Angeles (UCLA): "We get in condition, learn fundamentals, and play together." With that formula—and some very talented players—

Wooden guided the Bruins to a record seven consecutive NCAA championships from 1967 through 1973 and ten overall.

Known as "the Wizard of Westwood," Wooden won his first national title in 1964, as

UCLA went 30–0. The school had several more undefeated years, including the 1966–1967 season, when the Bruins were led by sophomore center Lew Alcindor, known today as Kareem Abdul-Jabbar. UCLA, however, reached the height of perfection from 1971 to 1974, when the team won eighty-eight games in a row.

The Streak Begins

Entering the 1970–1971 season, the Bruins had lost Alcindor, but they had another all-American, senior forward Sidney Wicks. With four national titles in a row, UCLA was a favorite to win the championship again. The Bruins started the season 14–0, then traveled to South Bend, Indiana, to play Notre Dame. UCLA had not lost to a team outside their conference in forty-eight games. The Fighting Irish, however, were not intimidated. Led by high-scoring guard Austin Carr, Notre Dame won 89–82.

Legendary UCLA coach John Wooden. His unequaled records as a college coach include an astonishing eighty-eight consecutive victories, seven straight and ten total NCAA championships, and thirty-eight straight NCAA tournament-game wins.

Their next game, the Bruins returned to the winning track, beating the University of California at Santa Barbara. UCLA finished the season without another loss and defeated Jacksonville for the NCAA championship. When the next season began, Bill Walton, another talented center, was ready to help the team. Wooden said, "If you were grading a player for every fundamental skill, Walton would rank the highest of any center who ever played." A sophomore, Walton averaged 21.1 points and 15.5 rebounds per game and was named the national college player of the year. The 6-foot-11-inch (211-cm) center led the Bruins to a 30–0 record. That year, UCLA won their games by an average of 30.3 points.

The next season was more of the same. Walton averaged 20.4 points and 16.9 rebounds per game. He was named player of the year, and UCLA had another 30–0 record. Against Notre

The box score for UCLA's 71–70 loss to Notre Dame

UCLA	FGA	FGM	FTA	FTM	REB	PTS
T. Curtis	11	3	4	3	1	9
P. Trgovich	5	3	1	1	0	7
B. Walton	14	12	0	0	9	24
D. Meyers	10	5	2	0	7	10
K. Wilkes	16	6	7	6	5	18
G. Lee	0	0	2	2	0	2
M. Johnson	0	0	0	0	0	0
Totals	56	29	16	12	27	70

Notre Dame	FGA	FGM	FTA	FTM	REB	PTS
G. Brokaw	16	10	7	5	3	25
D. Clay	5	2	4	3	6	7
J. Shumate	22	11	4	2	11	24
A. Dantley	12	4	1	1	8	9
G. Novak	2	0	0	0	0	0
B. Paterno	4	2	0	0	1	4
R. Martin	1	1	0	0	2	2
Totals	62	30	16	11	31	71

Dame, the Bruins broke the record for consecutive wins—sixty—set by the University of San Francisco during the 1950s. Entering the 1973–1974 season, the Bruins' winning streak was at seventy-five, and people wondered how long it could last.

Notre Dame Again

UCLA started the new season with thirteen straight wins. The last, against Iowa, was a 68–44 romp. On January 19, 1974, the Bruins returned to South Bend, where almost three years before they had lost their last game. Once again, the Fighting Irish were up to the challenge of playing the nation's best team. Walton looked forward to the game, too. He sat out several games because of a back injury, but he was ready to play that day in Indiana. He later wrote, "Of all the college teams I played against, Notre Dame was the one I wanted to beat most."

The Irish strategy was to press UCLA, force turnovers, then feed the ball to its all-American, John Shumate. The Bruins relied on Walton and forward Keith Wilkes for its offense. At halftime, UCLA was up by nine, and with 3:38 to go it held an eleven-point lead. In those last few minutes, however, Notre Dame stepped up

Bill Walton brought leadership as well as talent to UCLA.

its defense and went on a twelve-point run. The last basket, from Dwight "Iceman" Clay, gave Notre Dame a 71–70 lead with just a few seconds to play.

With Walton covered, UCLA worked the ball to Tommy Curtis. He missed, but UCLA controlled the rebound. Another shot, another miss. After the ball went out of bounds off Notre Dame, Walton took a pass, shot, and missed. The Bruins frantically scrambled to tip in the rebound. Finally, Shumate grabbed the ball as the clock ran out. Notre Dame had ended the longest winning streak ever in NCAA basketball.

Walton lets a jumper fly in the fateful game against Notre Dame that ended the Bruins' winning streak.

UCLA won some revenge the following week, when it defeated the Irish at home. The season, however, ended with another broken streak, as UCLA failed to reach the finals of the NCAA tournament for the first time since 1967. The Wizard of Westwood and his team had run out of tricks—at least for that season.

THE WIZARD'S WORDS

After the loss at Notre Dame, John Wooden offered his views on the game and the winning streak:

I honestly have no feelings either way about our winning streak being ended. I've said at least 100 times that once we broke the record for consecutive victories, the length of the streak was meaningless. The important thing was breaking the consecutive record.

The most disappointing thing for me about our losing was our inability to score in those last 3 1/2 minutes. I don't think I've ever had a team in a game give up 12 points like that in the last few minutes without scoring itself. . . .

Although the streak was meaningless to me, personally, I don't think there's any doubt but what the very existence of the winning record gave great interest to college basketball.

KAREEM ON TOP

Kareem Abdul-Jabbar Sets the Career Scoring Record

As Lew Alcindor, he dominated college basketball and led the UCLA Bruins to three straight national championships. As Kareem Abdul-Jabbar—an Arabic name meaning "noble, powerful servant"—he set more than twenty NBA records, with many still standing. By any name, he was one of the greatest players ever to step on a basketball court.

Then known as Lew Alcindor, Kareem Abdul-Jabbar helped UCLA win three national championships.

At 7 feet 2 inches (219 cm) and 267 pounds (121 kg), Abdul-Jabbar lacked the muscular build of a Wilt Chamberlain or Shaquille O'Neal. He did, however, have grace and a soft shooting touch. His trademark was the skyhook—a short, leaping hook shot over the defense. But Abdul-Jabbar was more than a scorer. He could also rebound and block shots, and he knew how to win. In the pros, he played on six championship teams and was twice named the MVP of the NBA finals.

Dominating from the Start

In 1969, when he was still known as Lew Alcindor, Abdul-Jabbar was the first player selected in the NBA draft, going to the Milwaukee Bucks. He finished the year with 28.8 points and 14.5 rebounds per game

Kareem Abdul-Jabbar as a Milwaukee Buck, defending against a driving Norm van Lier of the Chicago Bulls in April 1974.

and easily won Rookie-of-the-Year honors. The next year, he led the NBA in scoring with 31.7 points per game—the first of four seasons he averaged more than thirty. He also led the Bucks to the league championship. After that season, Abdul-Jabbar took his new name to show his devotion to his faith, Islam.

Always near the league leaders in scoring and rebounds, Abdul-Jabbar played three more seasons in Milwaukee before going to the Los Angeles Lakers. By the early 1980s, the Lakers had one of the most potent NBA teams ever, as Abdul-Jabbar was joined by such talented players as Magic Johnson, James Worthy, and Michael Cooper. Abdul-Jabbar and Johnson led the Lakers to five championships in nine years.

With so many good players around him, Abdul-Jabbar did not have to dominate the offense. His scoring average slipped a bit in 1982–1983 and 1983–1984, as he hit new career

lows each season. Still, Abdul-Jabbar's lows were better than most players' highs, and during the 1983–1984 season, he was on track to break Wilt Chamberlain's record for most career points.

Kareem uses his agility and considerable physical presence to go up against the Indiana Pacers.

Setting the Mark

Abdul-Jabbar had entered the NBA as Chamberlain's career was coming to an end. Abdul-Jabbar later wrote that he had played extra-hard against "Wilt the Stilt": "If I hadn't, he would have dominated me, embarrassed me in front of the league, and undermined my whole game and career." The two centers were often compared, because of their size, their scoring talents, and their playing for the Lakers. In a way, it seemed fitting that Abdul-Jabbar was the man chasing Chamberlain's scoring record.

On April 5, 1984, the Lakers went to Nevada to play the Utah Jazz. At that time, the

BY THE NUMBERS

Kareem Abdul-Jabbar's major career offensive statistics

Season	G	FGM	FGA	PCT	FTM	FTA	PCT	REB	AST	PTS	RPG	APG	PPG
69–70/Bucks	82	938	1,810	.518	485	743	.653	1,190	337	2,361	14.5	4.1	28.8
70–71/Bucks	82	1,063	1,843	.577	470	681	.690	1,311	272	2,596	16.0	3.3	31.7
71–72/Bucks	81	1,159	2,019	.574	504	732	.689	1,346	370	2,822	16.6	4.6	34.8
72–73/Bucks	76	982	1,772	.554	328	460	.713	1,224	379	2,292	16.1	5.0	30.2
73–74/Bucks	81	948	1,759	.539	295	420	.702	1,178	386	2,191	14.5	4.8	27.0
74–75/Bucks	65	812	1,584	.513	325	426	.763	912	264	1,949	14.0	4.1	30.0
75–76/Lakers	82	914	1,728	.529	447	636	.703	1,383	413	2,275	16.9	5.0	27.7
76–77/Lakers	82	888	1,533	.579	376	536	.701	1,090	319	2,152	13.3	3.9	26.2
77–78/Lakers	62	663	1,205	.550	274	350	.783	801	269	1,600	12.9	4.3	25.8
78–79/Lakers	80	777	1,347	.577	349	474	.736	1,025	431	1,903	12.8	5.4	23.8
79–80/Lakers	82	835	1,383	.604	364	476	.765	886	371	2,034	10.8	4.5	24.8
80–81/Lakers	80	836	1,457	.574	423	552	.766	821	272	2,095	10.3	3.4	26.2
81–82/Lakers	76	753	1,301	.579	312	442	.706	659	225	1,818	8.7	3.0	23.9
82–83/Lakers	79	722	1,228	.588	278	371	.749	592	200	1,722	7.5	2.5	21.8
83–84/Lakers	80	716	1,238	.578	285	394	.723	587	211	1,717	7.3	2.6	21.5
84–85/Lakers	79	723	1,207	.599	289	395	.732	622	249	1,735	7.9	3.2	22.0
85–86/Lakers	79	755	1,338	.564	336	439	.765	478	280	1,846	6.1	3.5	23.4
86–87/Lakers	78	560	993	.564	245	343	.714	523	203	1,366	6.7	2.6	17.5
87–88/Lakers	80	480	903	.532	205	269	.762	478	135	1,165	6.0	1.7	14.6
88–89/Lakers	74	313	659	.475	122	165	.739	334	74	748	4.5	1.0	10.1
Totals	1,560	15,837	28,307	.559	6,712	9,304	.721	17,440	5,660	38,387	11.2	3.6	24.6

Jazz played several home games in Las Vegas. Abdul-Jabbar entered the game twenty points shy of Chamberlain's record of 31,419. He scored eighteen through the first three quarters, helping the Lakers build a fifteen-point lead. It seemed he could have gone for the record in the third quarter, but several times he decided to pass rather than shoot.

Early in the fourth quarter, Abdul-Jabbar took a pass from James Worthy and dunked, tying Chamberlain. Now the Lakers were eager to feed him so he could score again. Abdul-Jabbar tried a short shot and missed. Finally, with about nine minutes to go, Magic Johnson passed him the ball. With Jazz center Mark Eaton guarding him, Abdul-Jabbar faked right, spun to the left, and went up for a skyhook. The ball swished through the net, giving him the new scoring record.

Abdul-Jabbar finished the season with 1,717 points and an average of 21.5 per game. He played five more seasons, finally retiring in 1989 at age forty-two. His final point total: 38,387, a record that reflects both incredible skill and longevity—and one that may not be broken for many years.

Kareem Abdul-Jabbar with his MVP trophy in 1980. By the time he retired in 1989, Kareem had amassed an unsurpassed six regular-season MVP awards—three with Milwaukee and three with the L.A. Lakers.

A THING OF BEAUTY

In his autobiography, *Kareem*, Abdul-Jabbar talks about the skyhook:

I've done so well with it that some people think I invented the thing, which obviously isn't true—it's just that I was in the last generation to learn that shot. Most kids nowadays don't learn to play with their backs to the basket, and if you don't have your back to the basket you can't shoot a hook shot. . . .

I had the form and release of the hook by the time I was a freshman in high school, but my coach there didn't emphasize it. At UCLA, Coach Wooden made me shoot the hook hundreds of times daily. . . .

When the skyhook and I are working, the hook and I are one. I've been flattered to hear that [Boston Celtics star] Bill Russell once called it the most beautiful thing in sports.

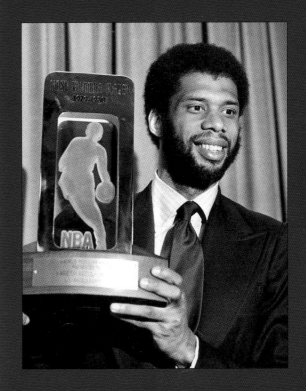

A MAGICAL DUO

The Magic Johnson/
Larry Bird Rivalry

They seemed so different: Magic Johnson, the flashy guard who oozed excitement, and Larry Bird, the quiet forward known as a "hick" from tiny French Lick, Indiana. Johnson played on the West Coast, Bird on the East. Johnson was black, Bird was white. Yet on a basketball court, they shared two things—amazing talent and a fierce desire to win.

The two stars first met on the court at the 1979 NCAA championship game. Earvin "Magic" Johnson was just a sophomore when he led the Michigan State Spartans to that title game. At 6 feet 9 inches (206 cm), Johnson was taller than other guards, yet he was still quick enough to defend

Magic Johnson was an energetic player and a crowd favorite.

shorter players. Bird, a senior, was the nation's second-leading scorer, and his Indiana State Sycamores entered the finals undefeated.

On March 26, the largest television audience ever to watch an NCAA basketball game saw Johnson dominate, as he scored twenty-four points and made laser-like passes to his teammates. Bird, stifled by the Spartan defense, made just seven of twenty-one shots from the floor.

Michigan State won, 75–64. Shortly after, Johnson announced he was turning pro. Bird was already slated to join the Boston Celtics. The two players knew their paths would cross in the NBA.

Another Finals Showdown

Drafted by the Los Angeles Lakers, Johnson brought an immediate spark to the team. The Lakers reached the NBA finals, winning the first three of five against the Philadelphia 76ers. For Game 6, Johnson moved from guard to center, replacing the injured Kareem Abdul-Jabbar. Johnson was brilliant, scoring forty-two points and grabbing fifteen rebounds. The Lakers won the series, and Johnson was named the MVP for the finals.

Meanwhile, in Boston, Bird brought his scoring touch with him to the pros, averaging 21.3 points his rookie season. Still, some people wondered if he had the moves to make it in the NBA. Bird said, "I admit I'm not the quickest guy in the world. In fact, I'm slow. But I've always tried to make up for it in other ways." Bird's other skills included

Bird and Johnson battle for the ball in an Indiana State–Michigan State matchup in 1979.

rebounding, passing, and hustling on every play. In 1980–1981, it was Bird's turn to help his team win a championship, as the Celtics beat the Houston Rockets.

As the 1980s went on, the Celtics and Lakers remained dominant teams, and Bird and Johnson were obviously the key players on their teams. "When we played the Celtics," Johnson wrote in his autobiography, "I was as emotionally high as I could possibly be. The basketball was just that good, and so was the competition."

Larry Bird, always cool under pressure, exuded confidence in his game.

The two stars finally met each other in a championship series in 1984. The Lakers reflected Johnson's style—quick and flashy—and were nicknamed "Showtime." The Celtics, like Bird, were a little slower, more physical, and always difficult to beat. The rivalry between the two players sparked extra interest in the series.

After four games, the series was tied at two games each. Playing in the Boston Garden, with the indoor temperature a steamy 97°F (36.1°C), Bird made fifteen of twenty shots and finished with thirty-four points, helping the Celtics win. The Lakers won the next game, forcing a decisive Game 7. With the Lakers trailing by three with about one minute to play, Johnson spotted teammate James Worthy under the basket. He never made the pass, however, as a Celtics defender knocked the ball away. The Celtics held on to win, and Bird was named the MVP of the series.

During the next three seasons, the Lakers and Celtics met two more times in the finals. In 1985, the Lakers beat the Celtics in Boston for the championship. Bird, meanwhile, won his second of three consecutive regular-season MVP awards. Johnson finally won his first in 1987 and then helped the Lakers beat the Celtics again for the NBA title.

Teammates and Hall Mates

The Bird/Johnson rivalry had cooled somewhat by then. The two men had become friendly, and now Michael Jordan was establishing himself as the premier pro player. Still, there was no doubt that Johnson and Bird had boosted the NBA's popularity with sports fans.

In 1991, Johnson's playing career was cut short when—to the shock of friends, fans, and other members of the sports community—he discovered he had the human immunodeficiency virus (HIV), the virus that causes AIDS. He briefly returned to basketball in 1992. He and Bird played together on the first "Dream Team," the first U.S. Olympic basketball team with NBA players. Johnson and Bird each averaged about eight points a game and helped the United States win the gold medal.

CAREER STATISTICS FOR LARRY BIRD AND MAGIC JOHNSON

Bird

G	MIN	FG%	3PT%	FT%	RPG	APG	PTS	PPG
897	34,443	.496	.376	.886	10.0	6.3	21,791	24.3

Johnson

G	MIN	FG%	3PT%	FT%	RPG	APG	PTS	PPG
906	33,245	.520	.303	.848	7.2	11.2	17,707	19.5

Larry Bird and Magic Johnson going head to head in June 1985.

Bird retired after the Olympics, though he coached the Indiana Pacers from 1997 to 2000. Johnson attempted a comeback in 1996, playing briefly for the Lakers, before retiring for good. In 1998, Bird was elected to the Basketball Hall of Fame, and Johnson joined him there in 2002, reuniting the two men who dominated basketball during the 1980s.

MUTUAL RESPECT

Magic Johnson and Larry Bird have often spoken of their respect for each other.

Johnson on Bird:

During my career in the NBA, I've gone up against hundreds, maybe even thousands of players. Many were good. A few were very good. A tiny handful even deserved to be called great. But there was nobody greater than Larry Bird.

Michael Jordan can do incredible things. . . . There's nobody like him. But Larry was the only player I ever feared . . . when we played the Celtics, no lead was safe as long as Bird was on the floor. . . . To most players, basketball is a job. To Larry, it was life.

Bird on Johnson:

I feel he's the greatest all-around team player in basketball. I have always looked up to him because he knows how to win. . . .

Both of us want to bring out the best in our teammates. We also want the fans to be involved in the game. Without them reacting, it just wouldn't be as much fun.

Magic plays to the strength of every teammate. The Lakers have a great team and they would be very good without him, but he is the special ingredient that brings them championships.

SCORES FOR THE PERFECT SEASON

UConn	Opponent	
93	Fairfield	50
91	Florida Int'l	47
94	North Carolina	74
69	Vanderbilt	50
84	Rhode Island	38
88	Wake Forest	38
103	Ball State	69
88	St. John's	28
97	Holy Cross	54
74	Louisiana Tech	50
86	Oklahoma	72
101	Cal State-N'ridge	44
84	Old Dominion	70
97	Wright State	39
112	Pitt	43
86	Tennessee	72
84	St. John's	43
96	Miami	50
85	Georgetown	41
93	Villanova	60
80	Notre Dame	53
79	Boston College	56
59	Virginia Tech	50
85	Providence	61
92	Seton Hall	40
77	Virginia Tech	42
85	Syracuse	55
106	Providence	41
80	Rutgers	42
89	West Virginia	60
78	Seton Hall	48
83	Villanova	39
96	Boston College	54
86	St. Francis	37
86	Iowa	48
82	Penn State	64
85	Old Dominion	64
79	Tennessee	56
82	Oklahoma	70

Huskies had an extra desire to win that game. After losing to the Huskies earlier in the season, an ODU player had said UConn was "beatable, very beatable." Bird had taped the quote in her locker and stared at it all season. After thirty-seven games, no one had found the key to making that prediction come true.

Two Steps to Perfection

The win over ODU gave UConn its third straight trip to the Final Four. In the national semifinals, UConn faced its old rival, Tennessee. Just as they had in the 2000 national championship game, the Huskies dominated the Lady Vols. Four of the five starters scored in double figures, and

Asjha Jones (15) and Diana Taurasi (3) of Connecticut fight Caton Hill of Oklahoma for a rebound in the NCAA finals.

Jones and Taurasi had ten rebounds each. After UConn's 79–56 win, Pat Summitt went to the Huskies' locker room and congratulated them. She later called Taurasi and Bird "the best offensive backcourt that I've seen in my twenty-eight years."

In the final, UConn played Oklahoma. The rematch presented some interesting stories. Auriemma had helped Sooner coach Sherri Coales get her job, and Oklahoma assistant coach Stacy Hansmeyer had played for Auriemma on the 2000 championship team. On the court, the Sooners had their own talented pair of guards, LaNeishea Caufield and All-American Stacey Dales. Auriemma insisted his team could be beat. "We have a lot of weaknesses, we really do," he said. "The problem is that it's hard for other teams to exploit them."

UConn showed some of those weaknesses once the game began. The Huskies turned the ball over often, and Bird and Taurasi struggled to hit outside shots. But with its strong inside game, the

Larry Bird and Magic Johnson going head to head in June 1985.

Bird retired after the Olympics, though he coached the Indiana Pacers from 1997 to 2000. Johnson attempted a comeback in 1996, playing briefly for the Lakers, before retiring for good. In 1998, Bird was elected to the Basketball Hall of Fame, and Johnson joined him there in 2002, reuniting the two men who dominated basketball during the 1980s.

MUTUAL RESPECT

Magic Johnson and Larry Bird have often spoken of their respect for each other.

Johnson on Bird:

During my career in the NBA, I've gone up against hundreds, maybe even thousands of players. Many were good. A few were very good. A tiny handful even deserved to be called great. But there was nobody greater than Larry Bird.

Michael Jordan can do incredible things. . . . There's nobody like him. But Larry was the only player I ever feared . . . when we played the Celtics, no lead was safe as long as Bird was on the floor. . . . To most players, basketball is a job. To Larry, it was life.

Bird on Johnson:

I feel he's the greatest all-around team player in basketball. I have always looked up to him because he knows how to win. . . .

Both of us want to bring out the best in our teammates. We also want the fans to be involved in the game. Without them reacting, it just wouldn't be as much fun.

Magic plays to the strength of every teammate. The Lakers have a great team and they would be very good without him, but he is the special ingredient that brings them championships.

BEST EVER?

UConn Women Go 39–0

Women's college basketball produced many fine teams before the 1990s, but few American sports fans paid much attention. In 1972, the Association of Inter-collegiate Athletics for Women (AIAW) held the first national college bas-ketball championship for women. Immaculata College won the first three titles, then Delta State took three in row. During the 1970s, Nancy Lieberman and Carole Blazejowksi—both future Hall of Famers—were among the stars in the women's game.

UConn's all-everything, Sue Bird, drives around Loree Moore of Tennessee in the 2002 finals.

In 1982, the NCAA held its first cham-pionship for women, won by Louisiana Tech. The next two years, the University of Southern California won, led by one of the foremost female players of all time, Cheryl Miller. The 1986 champs, Texas, went undefeated, and then Stanford and Tennessee emerged as the teams to beat.

Building a Rivalry

During the 1994–1995 season, a rivalry developed that sparked new interest in women's basketball. The University of Connecti-cut (UConn), coached by Geno Auriemma, beat top-ranked Tennessee on January 16 and then beat the Lady Volunteers a sec-ond time in the national championship game. UConn had a 35–0 record, the first time any college basketball team, men's or women's, won so many games during a perfect season. For the next several seasons, women's basketball fans eagerly awaited each UConn-Tennessee game, as the two programs remained among the best in the country.

Tennessee, coached by Pat Summitt, asserted its dominance the next three seasons, winning three straight national championships. The Lady Vols capped the run in 1998 with its own undefeated season, going 39–0. Two years later, Tennessee and UConn met again for the national championship. Once again, UConn came out on top. Injuries to key players hurt the Huskies during the next year's NCAA tournament, but in 2001, Auriemma's club was ready to go for its third national title, led by what many opposing coaches called the best starting five players ever in women's basketball.

The team featured four seniors: point guard Sue Bird and forwards Swin Cash, Tamika Williams, and Asjha Jones. They had come to UConn as one of the best freshmen classes ever. At first, however, Auriemma was not impressed. After a week of practice, he later said, "they didn't do anything." His assessment at the time: "They stink." But by their senior year, the four had developed into All-Americans, with Bird as the leader. In 2002, she was recognized as the national player of the year. The last starter, sophomore Diana Taurasi, was one of the most exciting young players in the game. She sank long threes as easily as she cut to the hoop, and her pinpoint passes sometimes stunned fans—and teammates not ready for them.

Road to the Championship

As the 2001–2002 season progressed, Connecticut demolished its opponents, winning by thirty or forty points per game. Its closest call came at Virginia Tech on January 29. At halftime, the Huskies led by three, and with just a few minutes to play, Virginia Tech tied the score at 48. In the

Connecticut's Swin Cash goes up for a shot as Michelle Snow of Tennessee defends during their semifinal matchup.

end, however, UConn pulled away for a 59–50 victory. With each win, more people began to wonder if UConn could match the 1997–1998 Tennessee team and go 39–0 on the way to another national championship.

The Huskies finished the regular season 33–0 and then swept the Big East conference championship. In the last game, UConn crushed Boston College, 96–54. Entering the NCAA tournament, Auriemma and his team were ranked number one in the nation, as they had been all season.

Sue Bird had averaged a little more than fourteen points per game in the regular season, but in the tournament she showed her scoring ability. Against Iowa, she led with twenty-two points and then poured in twenty-four against a tough Penn State team. In the regional finals against Old Dominion University (ODU), Bird had twenty-six points as UConn won 85–64. The

Huskies had an extra desire to win that game. After losing to the Huskies earlier in the season, an ODU player had said UConn was "beatable, very beatable." Bird had taped the quote in her locker and stared at it all season. After thirty-seven games, no one had found the key to making that prediction come true.

Two Steps to Perfection

The win over ODU gave UConn its third straight trip to the Final Four. In the national semifinals, UConn faced its old rival, Tennessee. Just as they had in the 2000 national championship game, the Huskies dominated the Lady Vols. Four of the five starters scored in double figures, and

Asjha Jones (15) and Diana Taurasi (3) of Connecticut fight Caton Hill of Oklahoma for a rebound in the NCAA finals.

Jones and Taurasi had ten rebounds each. After UConn's 79–56 win, Pat Summitt went to the Huskies' locker room and congratulated them. She later called Taurasi and Bird "the best offensive backcourt that I've seen in my twenty-eight years."

In the final, UConn played Oklahoma. The rematch presented some interesting stories. Auriemma had helped Sooner coach Sherri Coales get her job, and Oklahoma assistant coach Stacy Hansmeyer had played for Auriemma on the 2000 championship team. On the court, the Sooners had their own talented pair of guards, LaNeishea Caufield and All-American Stacey Dales. Auriemma insisted his team could be beat. "We have a lot of weaknesses, we really do," he said. "The problem is that it's hard for other teams to exploit them."

UConn showed some of those weaknesses once the game began. The Huskies turned the ball over often, and Bird and Taurasi struggled to hit outside shots. But with its strong inside game, the

Huskies managed to take a twelve-point halftime lead. In the second half, the Sooners cut the lead to six with just 2:22 to go. A few seconds later, Taurasi made what many considered the play of the game. She turned and hit a short jump shot while drawing a foul off of Dales. The foul was Dales's fifth, forcing her to leave the game.

With time running out, the Sooners needed to foul as soon as UConn touched the ball. The Huskies, however, managed to keep the ball in the hands of Bird, their best free-throw shooter. With about one minute to play, she hit two free throws to give the Huskies an eleven-point lead. Moving quickly up the court, the Sooners hit a three-point shot to cut the lead to eight. Bird made two more free throws to make the score 80–70. The Sooners tried to launch another three, but Tamika Williams blocked the shot. Bird then added two more points from the free-throw line. Oklahoma did not score again, and the Huskies were national champions.

All five UConn starters reached double figures, and the team out-rebounded Oklahoma by eighteen. The Huskies became the second team to go 39–0 and the first women's team to have two undefeated seasons. Afterward, Auriemma considered whether he had coached the best women's team of all time, as many people had said. "You can't say best ever, because it's a different era . . . different circumstances. We were the best team this year, by a little bit, over a really, really good team."

Rebecca Lobo reaching up to block a shot during a 1995 matchup against the University of Kansas.

THE FIRST PERFECT SEASON

All year long, the 2001–2002 UConn team heard it never could have beaten the 1994–1995 Huskies. That statement came from assistant coach Jamelle Elliot, a member of the 35–0 '95 squad. The lineup that year also included senior forward Rebecca Lobo, junior point guard Jen Rizzotti, and sophomore forward Kara Wolters.

The '95 team was good, but no one expected an undefeated season. UConn first won national recognition that year by defeating Tennessee in January. When the two teams met again in the NCAA final, however, Tennessee was favored to win. Lobo started well for UConn, scoring six of the team's first twelve points, but she soon found herself in foul trouble—and on the bench. At halftime, the Lady Vols led by six, and they held the lead for most of the second half. Lobo, however, stayed out of further foul trouble and got hot, grabbing key rebounds and scoring eleven points. Her free throws at the end of the game sealed the victory. Final score, 70–64 UConn.

AIR JORDAN SOARS AGAIN

Michael Jordan Wins His Sixth NBA Championship with the Chicago Bulls

From his first NBA game to his most recent, Michael Jordan has thrilled basketball fans with powerful dunks and smooth three-pointers. Known as "Air Jordan" and "His Airness," Jordan has appeared in movies, led the United States "Dream Team" to the 1992 Olympic gold medal, and become an international star.

Jordan shocked the world when he announced his retirement in 1993, after

Michael Jordan will long be remembered as one of the most effective, charismatic, and popular figures ever to grace the hardwood floors of the NBA.

leading the Chicago Bulls to three consecutive championships. He wanted to play baseball, he said, and given his athletic talent, he had a chance to fulfill that dream. After struggling in the minors, however, Jordan returned to basketball, where he was once again its king.

In 1996 and 1997, Jordan helped the Bulls win two more NBA titles. He also collected the MVP award for the finals each year, adding to the three he had already won. Entering the 1997–1998 season, Jordan prepared to give the Bulls another "threepeat," but questions swirled around the star and his team. Were Jordan and the Bulls too old to win again? Did Jordan have enough help on the court? Most important, to basketball fans—was this going to be Jordan's last season?

Still the Best

Jordan never said for sure if he would retire at the end of the season, but there were strong hints. Bulls coach Phil Jackson was feuding with Chicago's management, and he seemed sure to be gone the next year. Jordan said he would not play for another coach—"If Phil is out, then this is my last year."

Fans began to assume Jordan would retire, and they came out in record numbers to watch him play. The Bulls, however, struggled early in the season. Scottie Pippen, an all-star forward who had played beside Jordan on all the championship teams, missed the first half of the season. His return in January sparked the Bulls, and they finished the regular season tied with the Utah Jazz for the league's best record. Jordan had a typically great year—MVP of the All-Star game and the league's leading scorer with 28.7 points per game.

The Bulls cruised through the first rounds of the playoffs, beating the New Jersey Nets in three straight and taking four of five from the Charlotte Hornets. The Bulls faced a much

Throughout their years together in Chicago, coach Phil Jackson and Michael Jordan shared a strong relationship marked by mutual support and loyalty.

tougher test in the semifinals against the Indiana Pacers. Jordan had called the Pacers a "speed bump" on the way to the finals, but Indiana almost derailed the Bulls. Led by Reggie Miller, the Pacers forced the Bulls to seven games. Chicago took the last game 88–83, with Jordan scoring twenty-eight points, grabbing nine rebounds, and making eight assists.

The Final Finals

Jordan and the Bulls met the Utah Jazz in the finals. The Jazz relied on two superstars for their power: John Stockton and Karl Malone. In their mid-thirties, they were old by basketball standards, but they were also smart and talented. The Jazz were also rested, as they had beaten the Los

"Air Jordan" hits a slam dunk against the Utah Jazz in the 1998 NBA finals.

Angeles Lakers in four straight while the Bulls were slugging it out with the Pacers.

In Game 1, Utah led after three periods, but the Bulls forced the game into overtime. Stockton scored Utah's last four points to seal an 88–85 win for the Jazz. Jordan scored thirty-three, but just thirteen in the second half. Jordan

and the Bulls bounced back in Game 2, winning 93–85. This time, Jordan excelled at the end, scoring thirteen points in the last quarter. After the game, Jordan said, "I feel good about our chances. I feel confident."

The Bulls won the next two games. One was a forty-two-point blowout, the other a four-point squeaker. Jordan led his team in scoring both games. Needing just one more win for the title, the Bulls fell short in Game 5. Trailing by one point with just seconds to go, Jordan launched a three-pointer—and missed. Utah hung in for the win and then, trailing in the series three games to two, still had a chance to even the series.

In Game 6, the Jazz led after each of the first three periods, but never by more than five points. Pippen sat out almost half the game because of a bad back, but Jordan played his best offense of the postseason. He scored twenty-three in the first half, and as the game wound down, he once again led the way. With the Bulls losing by three, Jordan drove for a layup, closing the gap to one point. On defense, he snuck in behind Malone and stole the ball. "Karl never saw me coming," he said later.

BY THE NUMBERS

Michael Jordan's statistics for Game 6 of the 1998 NBA finals

MIN	FGM	FGA	FTM	FTA	REB	AST	PTS
44	15	35	12	15	1	1	45

Just under 19 seconds remained in the game. Jordan slowly brought the ball up court, and then, with 6.6 seconds to play, he jumped and shot. The ball sailed through the net, giving the Bulls an 87–86 lead, and they held on for the win. The Bulls were champions again, and Jordan won his sixth finals MVP trophy.

Just a few months later, it seemed that Jordan's game-winning jumper would be the last NBA shot he'd ever take. In the fall of 1998, a labor dispute between the players and owners delayed the start of the season. When play finally began in 1999, Jordan announced his retirement. But Jordan was unable to cut himself off completely from the game he loved, and in 2000 he became part owner of the Washington Wizards. Eventually, even that wasn't enough for His Airness. In 2001, he announced his decision to play for the Wizards.

Some basketball fans criticized the move. They wanted Jordan's heroics in the 1998 championships to be their last memory of this basketball legend. But Jordan felt the need to compete once again. "I'm all about challenges and seeing if I can go out and see if I can achieve something," Jordan said. "If at the end of the day I do it, great. If I don't, I can live with myself." Jordan's return brought some excitement to the NBA, even if his play was not as sharp as it had once been. And no matter what he did with the Wizards, no one could ever erase Jordan's six championship seasons with the Bulls.

THE WINNING PLAY

After Game 6, Michael Jordan described the last seconds of the game:

When I got the ball, I looked up and saw 18.5 seconds left. And I felt like we couldn't call a time-out; it gives the defense an opportunity to set up. It was a do-or-die situation. I let the time tick to where I had the court right where I wanted it. Great look [at the basket]. And it went in.

I saw the moment, and I took advantage of the moment. I never doubted myself.

Jordan reacts with a mixture of joy and pure adrenaline after the Bulls win Game 6 against the Jazz on June 14, 1998.

FOUR FOR FOUR

The Houston Comets Win the First Four WNBA Championships

Professional women's basketball leagues had come and gone before the Women's National Basketball Association played its first game in 1997. The WNBA, however, had some advantages the old leagues lacked: the financial support of the NBA and the biggest stars of the women's game.

One of these stars was Sheryl Swoopes. At the 1996 Summer Olympics, she helped the U.S. women's basketball team win the gold medal. After the Olympics, she joined the WNBA and went to the Houston Comets. Swoopes sat on the sidelines most of the 1997 season, having given birth in June. Her teammates, however, did fine without her.

Led by Cynthia Cooper, the league's leading scorer, the Comets finished first in the Western Conference. Cooper, who had played as a pro in Europe, was named the league's MVP, and she set a scoring record with forty-four points in one game. In the championship game against

Leading scorer Cynthia Cooper taking on the Los Angeles Sparks.

the New York Liberty, Cooper once again carried the play. She scored twenty-five as the Comets beat New York 65–51.

Ready for More

The next season, with Swoopes playing at full strength, the Comets came out ready to defend the WNBA title. Along with Cooper and Swoopes, Houston had another all-star, forward Tina Thompson. The Comets roared through the regular season, finishing 27–3. Coach Val Chancellor praised his team's effort. "They don't always play well," he said. "They don't always make their shots, but they always play hard."

A dominating Sheryl Swoopes proved to be a key ingredient in the success of the Houston Comets.

In the playoffs, the Comets swept the Charlotte Sting, despite minor injuries to Cooper, Swoopes, and guard Kim Perrot. In the first game of the finals against the Phoenix Mercury, the Comets lost, 54–51. Playing a best-of-three series, the Comets knew they had to do better in Game 2. With about seven minutes to go, Houston trailed by twelve, and Phoenix seemed ready to claim the second WNBA championship. Cooper then took over for the Comets, leading an amazing comeback and forcing the game into overtime. Houston finally won, 74–69.

The final game was close most of the way, until Swoopes began to dominate late in the second half. Rebounding, scoring, blocking shots—she did it all as Houston pulled away and won 80–71. Afterward, Swoopes was happy she had played such an important role in the Comets' victory, since her first season had been cut short. She added, "I look forward to doing it again."

The odds seemed good for the Comets to win a third championship, since they returned with all their stars from the 1998 team. Houston once again dominated during the regular season, losing just one game at home and finishing with a 26–6 record. The season's biggest difficulty was dealing with the death of Kim Perrot, who had been diagnosed with cancer in February. The Comets dedicated their quest for a "threepeat" to her.

For the third straight year, Cooper was the league's leading scorer and MVP. In the playoffs, the Comets took two out of three from the Los Angeles Sparks, then faced the Liberty in the finals. After an easy win in Game 1, Houston fans prepared to celebrate their third WNBA championship. Their hopes fizzled, however, when Teresa Weatherspoon hit a 50-foot (15.3-m) miracle shot at the buzzer that won the game for New York. But in the final game, Cooper led the offense, scoring twenty-four, and the Comets' defense shut down the Liberty. An emotional Houston team celebrated their third title, happy they could win it for Perrot.

Tammy Jackson and New York Liberty player Sue Wicks in a tussle for the ball during the 2000 championships.

Rare Ground

In 2000, Houston looked strong enough to win a fourth title. The Comets had an easy time during the regular season, going 27–5, and Swoopes was named the MVP. Before the playoffs, Cooper announced that she would retire at the end of the season. Sacramento Monarchs coach Sonny Allen said, "I hope she keeps her word." That comment came after Cooper had scored twenty-five points in the Comets' 72–64 victory over the Monarchs in the first playoff game. Houston finished off Sacramento then won a playoff

BY THE NUMBERS

Highlights of the Houston Comets' four championship seasons

98–24 regular-season record

16–3 postseason record

Three league MVPs (Cooper 1997–1998; Swoopes 2000)

Four Finals MVPs (Cooper 1997–2000)

Three WNBA Coach of the Year awards (Chancellor 1997–1999)

One WNBA All-Star Game MVP (Thompson 2000)

series over Los Angeles, putting them in the finals against the Liberty.

In Game 1, New York kept the game close and trailed by just four with less than a minute to play. Cooper, however, made a key three-point play with just twenty-six seconds left, sealing the win. She said afterward, "I really felt like I had to take it upon myself to be the leader in that situation." In Game 2, the Liberty led with just seconds to play, but Cooper sank a three-point shot that tied the game. She then scored six points in overtime to give the Comets the championship. For the fourth consecutive year, Cooper was named the MVP of the finals.

Even without Cooper, the Comets made a run at a fifth championship in 2001 but lost in the first round. Still, with its four titles, the team had secured its place in sports history. The Comets became just the second professional basketball team to win four or more consecutive championships, and the fifth in any major professional sport to achieve that feat.

Cynthia Cooper and Tammy Jackson sharing the fun after winning their third WNBA championship.

A GREAT ENDING

After helping the Comets win four straight WNBA championships, Cynthia Cooper addressed the Houston fans:

I came in and . . . nobody knew me. I worked hard, every single game I left my heart and my soul out on the court. For all four seasons I really demonstrated that I want to promote women's basketball. I love women's basketball and I come out and play with a passion that any and everybody should come out and play with, and the result of that is four championships . . . and you know what, you couldn't ask for a better ending to this story.

SHAQ ATTACKS IN THE NBA FINALS

Shaquille O'Neal and Kobe Bryant Lead the Lakers to Three Straight League Championships

Take the most agile big man in the NBA. Pair him with a talented young star who reminds people of Michael Jordan. Add a successful coach known for getting players to accept their roles and play as a team. The result: back-to-back-to-back NBA titles.

The Los Angeles Lakers used that recipe to establish themselves as the first great NBA

Shaquille O'Neal, the quintessential NBA big man and driving force on the Lakers.

team of the twenty-first century. With Shaquille O'Neal dominating at center and Kobe Bryant shooting and passing with flair, the Lakers won the title in 2000. In 2001, they defended the championship with an incredible 15–1 postseason run, giving them the best winning percentage ever in the NBA playoffs. In 2002, they made it a "three-peat" in a four-game sweep of the upstart New Jersey Nets. Throughout it all, coach Phil Jackson won credit for keeping his two stars and the rest of the Lakers playing at such a high level when it counted most.

Rebuilding a Winner

The Lakers were among the NBA's best teams during the 1980s, winning five championships. By 1992, however, the team had lost its major stars—including Kareem Abdul-Jabbar and Magic Johnson—and struggled in the playoffs. In 1996, the Lakers took two big steps toward regaining their past success when they got O'Neal from Orlando and drafted Bryant.

At 7 feet 1 inch (216 cm) and 315 pounds (143 kg), "Shaq" entered the league in 1992 and immediately made his large presence felt, winning the Rookie of the Year award. With his size, he easily positioned himself for basket-shaking dunks. With his rebounding and shot-blocking skills, he was also a force on defense. Each season, O'Neal improved, and by the time he joined the Lakers, he was the league's top center.

Bryant, a 6-foot-7-inch (201-cm) guard, had skipped college and joined L.A. when he was eighteen. The son of a former NBA player, he had spent much of his childhood in Italy before settling in Pennsylvania, where he set high-school scoring records. Bryant emerged as a starter with the Lakers in 1998 and finished the 1998–99 season averaging almost twenty points a game.

Even with O'Neal and Bryant, the Lakers

Kobe Bryant puts on the moves to get past Indiana's Reggie Miller in the 2000 NBA finals against the Pacers.

did not recapture their old form until Jackson arrived in 1999. As coach of the Chicago Bulls, Jackson had convinced Michael Jordan to lower his scoring totals and adopt a new offense. All the Bulls accepted Jackson's approach, and the team won six league titles in eight years. In Los Angeles, Jackson did something similar. He asked Bryant to shoot less and involve the other players more. On defense, he had the whole team step up its game. The Lakers finished the 1999-2000 regular season with a 67–15 record and reached the NBA finals for the first time since 1991.

Derek Fisher had his hands full trying to block Allen Iverson of the Philadelphia '76ers in Game 5 of the 2001 NBA Finals.

A New Dynasty?

The Lakers faced the Indiana Pacers for the title. In the first game, the Lakers won easily, 104–87, as O'Neal scored forty-three. In Game 2, Bryant went out with an ankle injury, but other Lakers helped fill the gap, and the Lakers won again. The next game, with Bryant still injured, the Pacers won 100–91, despite thirty-five points

from O'Neal. Bryant was back for Game 4, and he took control when O'Neal fouled out. After L.A. won in overtime 120–118, O'Neal said of Bryant, "He's the hero of the game, and I'm just glad I'm part of this legendary one-two punch."

The Pacers won the next game, but the Lakers came back with a knockout in Game 6, winning 116–111. O'Neal averaged forty-one points and twelve rebounds per game for the series and was named the MVP.

With Shaq and Kobie still improving, L.A. was favored to repeat as champs in 2001. During the season, however, the two feuded. Each wanted to be the "go-to" player. In the playoffs, the tension finally broke. After beating San Antonio in the first game of the Western Conference finals, O'Neal called Bryant "my idol." Bryant called O'Neal "the most dominant player in the league," adding, "Winning obviously brings up the spirits of everybody on the team."

The Lakers were certainly winning. Before the San Antonio series, they had beaten the Portland Trailblazers three straight. Against the

SHAQUILLE O'NEAL'S AND KOBE BRYANT'S MAJOR STATISTICS FOR THE 2002 NBA FINALS

G	FGA	FGM	FG%	3PTA	3PTM	3PT%	FTA	FTM	REB	AST	AV PTS
					O'Neal						
4	84	50	.595	0	0	0	68	45	62	15	36.25
					Bryant						
4	70	36	.514	11	6	.545	36	29	26	21	26.75

Sacramento Kings in a best-of-seven series, the Lakers won four in a row; then they beat the Spurs in four games to reach the finals. Their opponents were the Philadelphia 76ers, led by high-scoring guard Allen Iverson.

In Game 1, the 76ers finally ended the Lakers' post-season streak, winning 107–101. From then on, the Lakers were in control. In Game 2, O'Neal dominated. He scored twenty points, grabbed twenty rebounds, handed off nine assists, and tied an NBA finals record with eight blocks. L.A. won, 98–89. Bryant led the way in Game 3, scoring thirty-two as forward Robert Horry poured on twelve points in the fourth quarter to seal a 96–91 Lakers victory. The Lakers won the next game, 100–86, as O'Neal scored thirty-four points. In Game 5, Rick Fox and Derek Fisher helped O'Neal and Bryant with the scoring, and the Lakers led by nineteen in the fourth quarter. Philadelphia fought back to within seven, but the Lakers held on for the win—and their second straight NBA title.

In 2002, L.A. barely beat Sacramento in their grueling seven-game Western Conference finals. In the NBA finals, they swept the Nets in four straight—and made history. Phil Jackson won his *third* "threepeat" (his first two were with Chicago), tying Boston's Red Auerbach for most NBA titles with nine. O'Neal set a four-game-finals scoring record (145 points) and won his third straight finals MVP. Clearly, the Lakers have established themselves as a team for the ages.

MORE TO COME

After Game 5 of the 2001 finals, Los Angeles Lakers coach Phil Jackson had these thoughts on Shaquille O'Neal:

He kept motivating the team. He kept his engines going. He kept conditioning and reconditioning himself, taking a lot of time with free throw shots and all the things that are the weak points of his game that he wanted to improve, and I think everybody just took his leadership this year as a big plus. Shaq, a lot of times, has not been as obvious a leader as he was this year. He truly was a great leader on this team.

And for him to win the second one, I think this is a validation of your greatness, your ability. You look back at your great centers that have been in this league, Chamberlain had two championships spaced apart for four, five years. Shaq has got more in him. I expect him to have more than two championships before he's finished with this game.

Shaq has plenty to celebrate: the Lakers' 2000 NBA championship and his personal MVP honors.

Basketball Time Line

1891   James Naismith invents basketball in Springfield, Massachusetts.

1939   The National Collegiate Athletic Association (NCAA) holds its first men's basketball tournament.

1946   The Basketball Association of America forms. Three years later, the league changes its name to the National Basketball Association (NBA).

1951   The NBA holds its first All-Star game.

1954   The NBA introduces the shot clock.

1959   The Boston Celtics win the first of eight consecutive NBA championships.

1962   On March 12, Wilt Chamberlain scores one hundred points against the New York Knicks; Oscar Robertson completes the season averaging double figures in points, rebounds, and assists.

1967   The American Basketball Association (ABA) forms to compete against the NBA.

1974   On January 19, the University of California at Los Angeles loses for the first time in eighty-nine games, ending the longest winning streak ever in college basketball.

1976   The ABA folds, and four of its teams join the NBA.

1979   Magic Johnson and Larry Bird face each other for the first time, at the NCAA championship game.

1982   The NCAA holds its first women's basketball tournament, which Louisiana Tech wins.

1984   On April 5, Kareem Abdul-Jabbar sets a new record for career points, breaking the mark set by Wilt Chamberlain.

1987   The NBA hosts its first exhibition games with foreign teams.

1992   Magic Johnson and Larry Bird play together on the U.S. Olympic basketball team and win gold medals.

1995   The University of Connecticut women's basketball team wins the national championship with a record of 35–0.

1997   The Women's National Basketball Association forms, and the Houston Comets win the first league title.

1998   Michael Jordan leads the Chicago Bulls to their third straight NBA championship and sixth in eight years.

2000   The Houston Comets win their fourth consecutive WNBA title.

2002   Shaquille O'Neal and Kobe Bryant help the Los Angeles Lakers win their third consecutive NBA title.

To Learn More

BOOKS

Lannin, Joanne. *A History of Basketball for Girls and Women: From Bloomers to Big Leagues.* Minneapolis: Lerner Sports, 2000.

Lovitt, Chip. *Michael Jordan*. Revised edition. New York: Scholastic, 1999.

Pietrusza, David. *The Boston Celtics Basketball Team.* Springfield, N.J.: Enslow, 1998.

Pro Sports Halls of Fame: Basketball. Danbury, Conn.: Grolier, 1997.

Sachare, Alex. *The Basketball Hall of Fame's Hoop Stats and Facts*. New York: J. Wiley, 1998.

Ungs, Tim. *Shaquille O'Neal*. New York: Chelsea House, 1999.

Wrobel, Scott. *Wizards of Westwood: The UCLA Bruins Story.* Mankato, Minn.: Creative Education, 1999.

INTERNET SITES

Basketball Hall of Fame
www.hoophall.com
For information on all the players, coaches, and officials in the Hall of Fame, along with a description of how members are elected and news on events at the hall.

NBA
www.nba.com
Includes league news, player profiles, scores, and links to every team.

WNBA
www.wnba.com
For news, profiles, scores, and links to every team.

NCAA Basketball
www.ncaabasketball.net/theGame.asp
For information on rules, statistics on some of the best college players ever, and current news.

The Vault – Basketball
www.tsn.sportingnews.com/archives/basketball.html
From the Sporting News, a look at some of the greatest moments in professional and college basketball, including a history of the NBA finals and the NCAA Final Four.

Index

ABOUT THE AUTHOR

As an editor at Weekly Reader *for six years, Michael Burgan created educational material for an interactive online service and wrote on current events. Now a freelance author, Michael has written more than thirty books, primarily for children and young adults. These include biographies of Secretary of State Madeleine Albright, Presidents John Adams and John F. Kennedy, and astronaut John Glenn. His other historical writings include two volumes in a series on American immigration and a series of four books on the Cold War. Michael has a bachelor of arts degree in history from the University of Connecticut and resides in that state.*